Noah's Park

HONK'S BIG ADVENTURE

Written by Richard Hays
Illustrated by Chris Sharp

A Faith Parenting Guide can be found on page 3.

Faith Kids®
is an imprint of Cook Communications Ministries,
Colorado Springs, Colorado 80918
Cook Communications, Paris, Ontario
Kingsway Communications, Eastbourne, England

HONK'S BIG ADVENTURE
©2000 by The Illustrated Word, Inc.

First printing, 2000
Printed in Canada
04 03 02 01 00   5 4 3 2 1

Digital art and design: Gary Currant
Executive Producer: Kenneth R. Wilcox

Faith
Parenting
Guide

Honk's Big Adventure

My child's need: To accept others as they are.

Biblical value: Acceptance

Learning styles: Help your child learn to accept others in the following ways:

Sight: Look back in the story and pick out some of the new animals that Honk met on his adventure. Why did he have trouble liking them or accepting them? Ask what your child does to accept and learn more about new people.

Sound: Read the story out loud and have your child read the parts where Honk is deciding that an animal he meets is not acceptable. Talk about how differences are a good thing and that God intended us to cooperate and get along and receive others with love, but not necessarily to feel that we all need to be just alike.

Touch: Pick out two of your child's favorite stuffed animals. Hold each one and talk about how they are different. Talk about how they are the same. Ask your child why they are favorites. What's special about each of them? Remind your child that each one of us is special in our uniqueness to God.

Dirt flew everywhere as Screech the monkey and Shadow the raccoon dug under a leafy willow tree. "This is going to be our best fort ever," Screech yelled as he pulled up a root and tossed it high into the air.

"Stop that, Screech," Stretch the giraffe called. She was trimming the dead branches off a tree to help it grow. "We need to care for our trees, not dig them up."

"Let them be, Stretch. We should all play today. It's the first day of spring," Ivory the elephant said as she sprayed water at Dreamer the rhinoceros. The two large animals romped in the pond splashing water at everything and everyone.

"Hey!" said a mud-covered Howler the lion. "Watch the water, Dreamer. You're spoiling my pineapple mudpack. I'm trying to give my mane golden highlights."

Ponder the frog looked up from planting flowers and laughed. "I think your mudpack would help my daisies more than your mane."

Into this whir-wind of activity walked Honk the camel. His purple fur was neat and clean, his hooves and teeth gleamed. Even the sparkle in his eye looked freshly scrubbed. Honk was dazzling. He stopped and looked around at the others. Screech and Shadow were covered with dirt. A coat of leaves clung to Stretch. Howler wore his pineapple mudpack. Even Ponder was almost buried in the soil as he planted his flowers. They were all dirty. Honk honked in disgust. He hated being dirty. *They're making a mess of our home, too,* he thought.

The clean camel looked up and saw Flutter the dove. At least Flutter was clean.

Honk approved of the way she stayed above the action. "Well, there's one other animal with some sense," he said as he looked into the pond and admired himself. Suddenly, Flutter dived into the pond and splashed mud and water all over Honk. Honk could not stand it any longer.

He stalked off.

The animals just laughed.

That afternoon, shiny as a new penny, Honk came back to the clearing. He carried a pack over his shoulder.

"You are all just too dirty," he announced. "I can no longer live in this muck. I must search for a home that is as clean as I am. Tomorrow I am leaving Noah's Park!"

"Wait, Honk," Ponder yelled. "You can't just leave, Noah's Park is your home!"

"Your friends are here, Honk,"
Dreamer added. "We've been
together too long to let a little
dirt come between us."

The others crowded around
the camel and tried to talk him
into staying, but Honk was
determined to leave.

With his nose
in the air,
he walked away.

The next day found Honk miles from Noah's Park. The sun shined brightly above him as he marched down the road. Birds chirped in the trees, and Honk whistled along. He thought for a moment about the grand home and agreeable new friends he would certainly find. He was a very happy and very clean camel.

He began to sing:

"I'm one good lookin' camel,
So clean and debonair.
From head to tail and back again,
I'm great, so please don't stare.

"I'm one good lookin' camel,
On that you can depend.
Just keep the dirt away from me,
No mud or slime, my friend.

"I'm one good lookin' camel,
No other can compare.
From polished teeth to shiny coat,
I even curl my hair.

"I'm one good lookin' camel,
Now on the road once more,
I'll find a place that's just for me,
And then I'll shut the door."

When the sun set, Honk realized that this was the first time he had ever been alone in the dark. As he tried to go to sleep, he heard strange noises from the forest and saw eyeballs staring at him from out of the night. Honk was very scared. He told himself that God would protect him, but he hid his head under his pack so he could get to sleep.

When the sun rose, Honk was in a tree, his legs splayed over the branches. He saw now that the eyes in the night were flowers with eye-shaped spots.

The flowers had
made the strange
noises he'd heard
as they blew
in the wind.
He was ashamed
of being
frightened,
but it was, after all, only the first night.

As Honk walked along the road, he decided he would find a new roommate first. Then the two of them could find a clean place to live. He soon spotted a skunk lying in a patch of flowers.

"I'm Honk," the camel introduced himself. "I'm looking for a new place to live."

"You can live here," said the skunk, pointing at the large hole in the ground. "Not many animals want to live with me. By the way, my name is Smelly."

"You certainly are," said Honk as he held his nose. Smelly even smelled worse than Dreamer, and Honk doubted that he was as smart as his rhinoceros friend.

Where the roads crossed, Honk met a fox named Brassy. She seemed very nice and very clean. But when Honk went to her home to meet her family, he learned that Brassy had ten little kits. In the blink of an eye, they had pulled Honk's tail, tripped him with a rope, smeared blueberries into his fine purple fur, and blew sneezing dust in to his face. They were worse than Screech and Shadow!

Over the next few days,
Honk met a goose,
a crocodile,
and a
warthog,
but none of the
possible roommates compared to his
friends in Noah's Park. They were
either noisy, dirty, or, in the case
of the warthog, just too ugly
to be around.

Why, wondered Honk,
did he like his old
friends better?

In the afternoon of the fourth day, Honk heard noises in the trees beside the road. Was someone following him? Nothing appeared, but the noise continued. Honk decided to hide in some bushes on the other side of the road. Soon, with the warm sun beating down, the tired camel fell asleep.

When Honk woke up, he was itching all over. He discovered that he had gone to sleep in a patch of poison ivy. Honk itched his way to a river where a rickety wooden bridge with a frayed rope was the only way to cross. When Honk stepped onto the bridge, it began to spin, tossing him into the water.

Now cold, wet, itchy, and still scared, Honk spent his fourth night huddled on top of a rock. A sharp hunger pang reminded him that his food supply was nearly gone.

Honk felt awful. Nothing was turning out the way he had imagined. Why was it so hard to find new friends? When he had lived in Noah's Park, none of the animals had seemed so wonderful, but now that he was gone, they all seemed to have things about them that Honk missed. He thought about tending the plants with Stretch, and skipping rocks with Ponder, and talking about his dreams with Dreamer. He even missed chasing Screech and Shadow after they had played one of their stupid tricks on him.

At least, he thought to himself, *I am clean*.
As this thought crossed his mind, a strong wind
from the east covered him with dirt and sand.

The next morning, Honk woke up no better off than the night before. He looked around the forest and finally found some bananas to eat. Yuck! They were mush! The food always seemed fresh in Noah's Park.

As he searched for
something else to eat,
he imagined what
his friends were doing
in Noah's Park.
He pictured Dreamer taking
a nap in warm Cozy Cave.
He thought about Ponder
floating on his lily pad.
He envisioned
Screech and Shadow
enjoying a meal
of blackberries
and mangos.
*Why am I thinking
about Noah's Park?*
Honk wondered.

After a meal of dandelions,
Honk continued his journey. He again heard noises
in the bushes, but this time he ignored them. B-I-I-I-G mistake!

Honk trudged along the road, still looking for food. He entered a
dark forest, hoping to find fresh fruit. He heard the noises again.
This time they were behind him. He spun around to catch the
noisemaker. It was a pack of evil-looking jackals.
They eyed him hungrily.

Honk kicked the closest jackal in the
nose. The jackal fell back into the others.
Honk ran out of the forest and
followed the road back.

The jackals raced up behind him. When he reached the winding river again, he jumped in, just escaping the snapping teeth of the jackals. Honk grabbed onto a log and let the swift river carry him along.

After a while he slept.

When Honk woke up,
he was still floating
in the water.
It was dark, but he could
hear a gentle waterfall
splashing in the distance.

Honk swam over and rinsed the muck and slime
off his coat. Then he ate a few bananas from the plentiful fruit trees.
Honk looked around. The air was clear. It even smelled clean.
This is a place I could settle down, he thought. This place had
everything: food, water, trees, a beach. What more could a
camel ask for? He would call it "Honk's Haven."
Satisfied with the thought, Honk fell asleep.

When Honk woke up, Ponder, Dreamer, Stretch, and all his other friends were there.

"Welcome home," said Ponder. "You look like you've had quite an adventure."

"Yes," answered a surprised Honk, "I have."

Honk realized that the river had carried him back to Noah's Park. "When I arrived here, it seemed like such a great place," Honk said. "It is," Ponder reminded him.

From that day forward Honk never left Noah's Park. He understood that his place in God's world was right there in Noah's Park. He appreciated his friends more and asked less of them. Of course, he did ask his friends if they could change the name of Noah's Park to Honk's Haven. The End.

DREAMER HAS A NIGHTMARE

Dreamer the rhinoceros loves to dream, until one day he has his first nightmare. How will Dreamer handle this frightening experience? Discover the answer in the Noah's Park adventure, *Dreamer Has a Nightmare*.

STRETCH'S TREASURE HUNT

Stretch the giraffe grew up watching her parents search for the Treasure of Nosy Rock. Imagine what happens when she finds out that the treasure might be buried in Noah's Park. Watch the fur fly as Stretch and her friends look for treasure in *Stretch's Treasure Hunt*.

CAMELS DON'T FLY

Honk the camel finds a statue of a camel with wings. Now, he is convinced that he can fly, too. Will Honk be the first camel to fly? Find out in the Noah's Park adventure, *Camels Don't Fly*.

DREAMER AND THE MYSTERY OF COZY CAVE

Dreamer the rhinoceros loves to dream. One day he dreams that there is a secret passage in Cozy Cave and then discovers it is real. He and his friends set out to explore the passage. Will they discover the mystery of Cozy Cave? Find out in the newest adventure from Noah's Park, *Dreamer and the Mystery of Cozy Cave*.

PONDER MEETS THE POLKA DOTS

Ponder the frog is growing lily pads in the Noah's Park pond. When something starts eating the lily pads, the normally calm frog decides to get even. Will Ponder save his lily pads? Find out in the colorful Noah's Park adventure, *Ponder Meets the Polka Dots*.